1

Victor smiled. He won the race! He always did. "Ivan, you're getting faster!" he joked.

Ivan tried to catch his breath. His hands were on his knees. "You really think so?" he joked back.

"Yes! You were close! Wasn't he, Carlos?"

Carlos shook his head. He bounced a soccer ball on his knee.

"Too bad you can't handle a soccer ball, Victor. Such a waste of speed."

"I use my speed," Victor said. "When the ladies chase me!"

"You got the looks, Victor. I'll give you that," Ivan said. He was still panting. "But not the brains."

Victor stopped smiling. That was low. Ivan knew it. Victor grabbed the soccer ball from Carlos. He threw it at Ivan. Ivan turned quickly. The ball hit his hip and rolled away.

It was hot in the park. The September sun was strong. Victor walked to the shade. Carlos joined him. Ivan walked to the soccer ball.

Carlos lit a smoke. He passed it to Victor. Carlos always shared.

Ivan returned with the ball.

Victor handed him the smoke. It was his apology for throwing the ball. Ivan accepted.

"So it is true?" Carlos asked. "About your sister Angela and Marcos?"

"It could be true," Victor said. "But she hasn't told my dad. So I don't know."

"Who is Marcos?" Ivan asked.

"You know," Carlos began. "That Puerto Rican. The student council guy."

"Oh," Ivan said. They all sat still. Ivan passed the smoke to Victor.

"Look on the bright side," Ivan said. "It's better than another white guy. Right, Victor?"

Victor took a long drag. "Barely,"

he said. "Let' s go. I can't be late for dinner."

2

The boys walked to Central Avenue. The stores there had Spanish signs.

Carlos could read them. Victor could not. He wanted to. But it was too late. He was seventeen. And he was flunking English. One language was enough.

Carlos and Ivan lived in the same building. Victor lived a few blocks away.

"*Hasta mañana*," Carlos and Ivan said.

"*Hasta mañana*," Victor replied. "See you tomorrow."

Victor walked home for dinner. His mom made a roast. The kitchen was so hot! They sat down at the table. Victor's dad said grace. Angela started right away.

"Guess what!" she said. "Marcos asked me to the dance! He's on student council!"

Their dad's fork stopped. "Good grades?" he asked.

"Very good grades! He's going to college, too!"

"He sounds great, Angie," their mom said. She tucked her blonde hair behind her ear. "But aren't you still seeing Edward? Did something happen?"

Angela didn't reply right away. Victor noticed. His fork stopped too.

"No, nothing. I just don't like him anymore. That's all."

"Dances are expensive," their dad said. "And you're already in cheerleading. I'll think about it, okay? Bring Marcos to meet the family first."

Angela beamed. "Thank you, Dad! You will love him. I know it!"

"Let's hope so," he said. "Speaking of grades. How's school so far, Victor?"

"Fine," Victor snapped. He didn't want his dad's opinion. Or a crummy job like his either. An airport translator? No way. Victor was going to work construction. Just like his grandpa had.

"I want you to graduate, Victor. That means no fights. And no Ds."

"I got it," Victor said. He stared at his plate.

3

Victor's mom woke him up. "It's Monday," she said. "Time for school."

He needed a shower. It was so hot yesterday.

"Keep the bathroom clean," his mom said. "Grandma comes tonight!" Victor hadn't seen Grandma for months. Not since Grandpa's funeral.

The bathroom door was locked.

Angela yelled, "I'm in here!" Victor heard the water running.

"So much for my shower," he thought.

At school Ivan came to Victor's locker. "Good morning, Your Highness," Ivan said.

Victor didn't listen. He couldn't find a pen. His locker was too messy. He gave up and slammed the door.

"I bet your old girlfriends all voted for you!"

"What the hell are you talking about?"

"You don't know? You are on the list for homecoming king! See those cheerleaders?" Ivan pointed down the hall. "They are hanging a banner. Guess whose name is on it? Yours."

Victor was shocked. His legs felt weak. He opened his locker. He pretended to look for a pen again.

"What does that even mean? What do I have to do?" Victor asked.

"You have to find a date. Find me one too, eh?"

Victor closed his locker. His heart was beating hard. It felt like track and field day. When he was a kid, he won ribbons. *Victor Hernandez. Winner. 100-meter dash.*

4

Carlos had an old Honda. He drove
Ivan and Victor home after school.

"You excited, Victor?" Carlos
asked.

Victor rolled his eyes. "Oh yeah. I
love school activities."

"Do you have a suit?" Ivan asked.
He was in the backseat.

"Not really," Victor said. Could
he rent one? No way. Too expensive.

Especially if Angela needed a dress too.

"What did you wear to your grandpa's funeral?" Ivan asked.

"I wore my dad's suit. Damn thing was small then. I'm bigger now."

"Hey, get this. Some black kid is on the list too!" Ivan said.

"I know him," Carlos said. "His name is Akil. His girlfriend is a basketball star."

That's another thing. Victor didn't have a date. He hung out with a lot of girls. But no one he would date. This whole thing was a mess.

Carlos stopped at Victor's. Victor was glad. He didn't want to talk anymore. He got out of the car. Ivan did too. He moved to the front seat.

"Hey, Victor," Ivan said. "Here comes Marcos and Angela."

"He's here to meet the family," Victor said.

"*Buena suerte, famo*," Carlos said. "Good luck, buddy." They drove away.

"Victor, wait up!" Angela yelled. Victor waited on the street.

"Hey, Victor," Marcos said. "I saw your name on the list. I hope you win. It's about time. You know, for some diversity."

Victor couldn't believe it. Who was this guy? Bonding over race?

"You heard that, huh? Well, I heard you are fast, Marcos. Fastest guy on the track team. Is that right?"

Marcos stepped forward. "You heard right, " he said.

"How about a race to Central Ave? One quick block?"

"Argh," Angela said. She sat on the stairs. "I'll count it off," she said.

The boys stood at a crack in the sidewalk.

"One. Two. Three!"

Marcos and Victor sprang forward. Victor usually took the lead early. But not this time. They were neck and neck!

Central Avenue was close now. Victor knew he had to dig in. There was a place deep inside him. It's where his speed came from. He didn't understand it. But he trusted it. He finished one-step ahead of Marcos.

Both boys panted. They nodded to each other. It was a sign of respect. They walked back to Angela.

Victor started up the stairs. "Now I really need a shower," he thought.

"Victor," Marcos gasped. "Why aren't you on the track team?"

Victor stopped. But he didn't turn around. "I don't have the right shoes," he said.

5

Victor turned off the shower.
He heard his grandma. She was
laughing with Angela. She's here!

He put a towel around his waist.
He ran quickly to his room. He got
dressed. He walked into the living
room.

"Hi, Grandma," he said.

"*Hola, guapo*!" Grandma said.

"Hello, handsome! Your sister told me! You might be king!"

"I doubt it, Grandma," Victor said.

Grandma lifted her eyebrows. "You've got the face for it!" She kissed his cheek. "It's good to see you."

The family went out to dinner. Angela helped Grandma read the menu. She told Grandma about Marcos too. She said some things in Spanish. Angela was good at languages.

Grandma raised her glass. "I am so proud of my *nietos*. My grandchildren," she said. "One met a nice young man. The other might be king!"

"A king with no date!" Angela joked.

Grandma frowned. "No date?"

Victor shrugged.

"If you could take anyone. Anyone in the whole school. Who would it be?" Grandma asked.

Angela almost told. But Victor spoke quickly. "I don't know, Grandma."

"You'll think of someone," Grandma said.

That night, Grandma slept in Victor's room. Victor was in Angela's room. He couldn't sleep.

"You awake?" he said.

"No," Angela said.

"Would she go with me, Ang? To the dance?"

"I told you before. Yes. Tiffany would go out with you."

Victor really liked Tiffany. No one knew except Angela. Not even Carlos or Ivan. They would tease him. Tiffany was the most popular girl at school.

"Victor, Marcos says you are fast," Angela said. "He says you're faster than he is!"

"Enough about Marcos. What the hell happened with Edward?"

"Argh! Nothing. Nothing bad. Don't fight with him. Okay, Victor? You've been so good. Nothing happened. Okay?"

"You're sure?"

"I'm sure."

"And you're sure Tiffany likes me?"

"Oh, go to sleep. Ask her yourself."

6

Victor woke up happy. Maybe he would ask Tiffany out. They were seniors now. Plus, Grandma was making *molletes*. They were so good! Victor ate a ton. Then he looked at the clock. He was late! He rushed to school.

First period was about to start. Victor raced to class. The halls didn't seem right. Everyone was on edge.

"Settle down," Ms. Burton said. "You might already know this. Someone wrote racist words on school property. If you know anything, tell me later. There is an assembly today in the gym."

Here we go again, Victor thought. Racist talk wasn't rare at Central. But he was glad about the assembly. It meant getting out of class.

The bell rang. Victor walked into the hall. He saw Ivan and Carlos.

"*Que pasa, famo*?" Carlos said. "How you doing, buddy?"

"Doing all right," Victor said. "Get this. I raced Marcos."

"I mean the banner, Victor."

"Huh?"

"The homecoming banner."

Carlos said. "Someone crossed off your name and Akil's. They wrote 'Vote White' on it."

Victor paused. "Is that what the assembly is for?"

"Yep," Carlos said.

"Well, I won't be there," Victor said. He walked right out of school. He couldn't go home. So he went to the park. He walked home at four o'clock. He acted like it was a normal day.

7

That night, Victor snuck out. He had a bottle inside his jacket. He knew it looked odd. Someone could notice. He might get busted. So he took side streets to the park.

Carlos and Ivan were there. "Did you get caught? For skipping?" Ivan asked.

"Hell no," Victor said. He opened the bottle.

By 1 a.m., the bottle was almost empty. Ivan was laughing. "I keep thinking about you. Up there with all those blancos! In a tiny suit!" he joked.

Victor grabbed the bottle. He took the last drink. "You won't see me up there, Ivan. Forget it." Victor looked at the empty bottle. He threw it up in the air. It flew over a parked car. It broke as it hit the street.

"What the hell is wrong with you?" Carlos said. Ivan didn't seem to care. He was still laughing.

"For real now," Ivan said. "Who wrote it? A *guero*? A white kid?"

"Shhhh," Carlos said. "Did you hear that?"

"Hear what?" Ivan said.

"A car door. Let's get out of here."

They started walking away. They heard a shout. "Hey! Stop right there!"

Carlos, Ivan, and Victor ran. Victor took the lead. He didn't stop. What else could he do? He ran all the way home.

Victor crept up the stairs. "I made it," he thought. But he was wrong. Grandma was awake. She sat at the kitchen table. She didn't look happy.

8

"Will you tell me where you were? Or should I wake your dad?" Grandma asked.

Victor sat down at the table. "I don't know where to begin," he sighed.

"Try the beginning."

"The beginning? Are you serious?"

Grandma nodded.

"Well, it started freshman year.

I wanted to try out for track. I was fast, Grandma. Remember track and field day? I won a lot of ribbons."

"I remember," Grandma said.

"So I needed track shoes. Dad took me to Goodwill. I found some really cool ones. They were red and yellow. They were hot."

"And?" Grandma said.

"It was the day of the tryouts. I took the shoes out of my bag. Edward said they were his old shoes. And they were, Grandma."

Grandma looked sad. "Children are mean, mijo. Especially about money."

"It's not just the money," Victor said. "They didn't want me on the team. If a white kid had used shoes, it wouldn't matter."

Victor put his head in his hands. "I tried to join them. It didn't work. Now it is happening again. But I didn't ask for it this time."

"Angie told me about the banner," Grandma said. "I'm so sorry."

"We don't belong here," Victor said. "Dad should have stayed in Mexico. Why didn't he work with Grandpa? Instead he married the first white woman he met."

"Enough!" Grandma said. She pounded her fist on the table. "You're thinking like a child."

She pointed her finger at him. "Listen to me, Victor," she said. "Your father married for love. Nothing else. Do you understand?"

Victor couldn't look up. Grandma stood up from the table. She walked away. Then she came back.

"Your dad has a gift, Victor. He loves languages. He decided to do what he loves. Do you think it was easy for him to leave? Victor and I," She stopped. "Your grandpa and I were glad."

Victor looked up. "Grandpa too?"

"Of course," Grandma said. "Life takes bravery, *mijo*. It's not easy to get the things you want."

Victor looked down again. He felt terrible. Grandma gave him a glass of water. She kissed the top of his head.

"That's enough for tonight, *mijo*. Get some sleep."

9

Victor woke up. Grandma and Mom were talking in the kitchen. Would Grandma tell on him?

Victor got dressed. He felt like a man on death row. He brushed his teeth. He walked to the kitchen.

"Good morning, Victor!" his mom said. "Grandma made *chilaquiles*! Help yourself, honey. I have to get to work. See you later."

Grandma sat at the table. She was drinking coffee. Victor sat across from her. "Thank you," he said quietly.

"*No pasa nada*," she said. "Nothing has passed. You should eat."

Grandma gave Victor a plate of *chilaquiles*. "A Mexican hangover cure," she said. She winked at him.

Victor ate all the *chilaquiles*. "You were right. I feel better!"

"I'm right about a lot things," she said. "Now you better get going."

Victor walked to the door. He put his hand on the knob. "Grandma," he said. "I'm going to get a date today. The one I want. And it won't be easy."

Grandma smiled. "Stars in your eyes. Just like your father!"

Victor walked as fast as he could. He wanted to find Carlos and Ivan. Did they make it home last night? Victor had no idea.

At school, he saw Carlos's car. His friends were in the hall. "You used your speed last night, eh, *famo*?" Carlos said.

"Man, am I glad to see you! " Victor said. "How did you get away?"

"With the help of an alley Dumpster," Ivan said. "It was lovely."

"You guys, I have a plan," Victor said. "It's a plan to save face. I'm going to get the prettiest girl in school. I'm going to ask Tiffany to the dance."

Carlos and Ivan were shocked. "*Tiene cruda*," Carlos said. "You're hung over. You're not making sense."

"I'll do it at the end of the day. Today. Watch me."

"Do you think she would? You know, go out with one of us?"

"We'll find out," Victor said. "I gotta get to class. Meet you in the parking lot after school?"

"Sure," Carlos said. "One more thing, Victor. My older brother has a suit you can wear. You two are the same size."

"Thanks, Carlos," Victor said.

The last bell rang. Victor went

to Tiffany's locker. She seemed surprised but happy to see him.

Victor took a deep breath. "Hi, Tiffany. Will you go to the dance with me?"

10

Victor ran to the parking lot. He felt great! Tiffany said yes! Things were looking up.

Victor saw Carlos and Ivan. They were by the car. Edward was nearby too. He was laughing with friends. "Don't look," Victor thought. But it was too late.

"Victor," Edward yelled. "I hear

you got some legs. That how you got across?"

Carlos and Ivan heard it. Victor could tell. What should he do?

He thought about hitting him. Victor could crush Edward. He had before. But what about those other guys? The ones Edward was with?

Carlos and Ivan would try to help. But they weren't fighters. Victor kept walking. He had to.

"Oh, wait. I forgot!" Edward yelled. "You aren't real Mexicans. You or your sister! What are you two? I'm so confused!"

Victor turned. To hell with it. Maybe he should hit him after all. His body was on fire.

"Victor!" someone yelled. It was Marcos. There was a man with him.

Edward walked away. "What a coward," Victor thought.

"Coach, this is Victor. The guy I told you about," Marcos said. "Victor, this is the track coach, Coach Perez."

"Nice to meet you, Victor," Coach Perez said. "And good luck getting voted king. You gotta ignore some folks in this school. Right?"

"I'm trying," Victor said. He looked back at Edward. "It's not easy. But I'm trying."